MW01243578

ROBERT ALDRIDGE *and* **MONA LONG**

October
ROSE

Celebrating a
Late Life Romance

Hope you enjoy reading of it as much as we enjoy living it

Robert & Mona

MCKINLEY BROWNE PUBLISHING

*We dedicate this book to our hair stylist
and friend, Maurice Rizzo, Jr., without whom
we might never have met. Thank you, Maurice.*

*Also, we thank our eight children,
who are very concerned with our happiness
and have graciously accepted the truth
of that old adage, "just because there is snow
on the roof doesn't mean there is no fire
in the furnace!"*

Preface

Are we really living longer or does it just seem longer? Is 70 the new 50, or is it the same old 70 with a face lift and tummy tuck?

Demographics show the fastest growing age group is the 100+ years category. What are we going to do with these bonus years? Are they a blessing or a curse? It depends on our outlook as much as our health.

We are two octogenarians (80s) who will share our story of late life romance with the hope we can help others find the joy of a twilight romance and also to challenge others to rekindle a present relationship.

One of the many things we have in common is a thirst for knowledge. My special lady has been active in establishing Lifelong Learning programs in Enid, Stillwater and Oklahoma City. Now I must confess my first experience with Lifelong Learning was primarily to spend more time with her and to share an activity that was so important in her life.

After that first series of classes, I was hooked. What a wonderful way to keep one's batteries charged! We meet new friends, learn new facts, and are exposed to new ideas. It sure beats watching daytime television. We like being with "inquiring minds" discussing events and ideas rather than dissecting the folks at the next table.

The writing class really struck a fire in me. It was for that class I wrote the poem "October Rose" that inspired this book, and we were challenged to prepare our story for publication as a part of our legacy.

– Robert Aldridge

October Rose was written for Mona in October
— three months after we met.

October Rose

Last night I took my dog outside for his bedtime bark.
There was a big harvest moon.
In the moon glow I noticed one lone rose
Blooming in my garden, one lone rose.

Naught is as lovely as the October rose,
Spilling its beauty 'neath the harvest moon.
Survivor of spring storms and summer drought,
Of insects that chew, aphids that suck and fungus that rots.
Now in solitary splendor spending that strength,
Perfuming the night air against winter's chill.

Our love is an October rose.
We have weathered the storms of youth,
The hectic years of acquisitiveness,
Been gnawed at by problems, sucked dry by disappointment,
Yet, now in the twilight of our lives,
We pour out our love for one another against the coming cold.

– Robert Aldridge

*Because so much of our relationship
revolves around music, we decided to use song titles
as chapter names. We had great fun selecting
these tunes. We hope they will stir your
memories as they do ours.*

Table of Contents

For more information or to book a public speaking engagement contact
McKinley Browne Publishing 405-513-1267.

ROBERT ALDRIDGE *and* MONA LONG

October ROSE

Celebrating a Late Life Romance

MCKINLEY BROWNE PUBLISHING

"Old Rockin' Chair's Got Me"

He says:

When one has exceeded the biblical three-score years and ten, there is a tendency to look backward...taking the scraps of a bruised ego, broken dreams, glory days and shining achievements, and cobbling them together into a castle of yesteryear, raising the drawbridge and waiting for the fire of life to grow cold.

I was at loose ends; my responsibility as caregiver was over. However, the gift of freedom had turned to ashes in my hands. I felt like some old relic washed up on the shore; a curiosity with lots of past but darn little future. I talked big about making a bucket list, but was increasingly mired in the sameness of days. Even a bucket list is focused on dying rather than living.

She says:

After several years of striving to keep a marriage intact, I decided to write the obituary for a marriage that was long dead. The years of denial, the years of staying for the children, the years of being resigned to my lot were over.

A marital therapist had shared a poem several years earlier and now its meaning became clear.

"Autobiography in Five Short Chapters"

Chapter I

I walk down the street.
There's a deep hole in the sidewalk.
I fall in.
I am lost… I am hopeless.
It isn't my fault.
It takes forever to find a way out.

Chapter II

I walk down the same street.
There is a deep hole in the sidewalk.
I pretend I don't see it.
I fall in again.
I can't believe I am in this same place.
But it isn't my fault.
It still takes a long time to get out.

Chapter III
I walk down the same street.
There is a deep hole in the sidewalk.
I see it there.
I still fall in…it's a habit…but,
My eyes are open.
I know where I am.
It is my fault.
I get out immediately.

Chapter IV
I walk down the same street.
There is a deep hole in the sidewalk.
I walk around it.

Chapter V
I walk down another street.

– Portia Nelson

I pondered these words. I met the truth. Two people had made dedicated attempts to salvage the remnants of a 58-year marriage. There was no energy left. It was time to pursue a healthier and peaceful life in the years remaining.

I moved to a new city to be near children and grandchildren. I was only Nana now. I loved the role...even though time and distance were leeching away the sweetness of cookie baker, confidant, and Dr. Nana who kissed the hurt away. Now I would be matriarch of the clan, secure in my new place. Guarded by my loyal children, I entered a new phase of life.

Day by day, week by week, choices were considered: gated area, condo or retirement center, new church, another bank, insurance changes, different doctors, establishing new friends, and facing the word divorce. After dealing with the emotions of grief, fear, and anxiety for a couple of years, I felt a renewed personal strength as my body was relieved of chronic pain. Belief in myself emerged. I began a life on my own.

"Memories"

She says:

"It was the best of times; it was the worst of times." Charles Dickens' famous line echoed around me. There I was, standing in the ashes of a long-time marriage, attempting to piece together shattered aspirations and dreams; however, bolstered by the stalwart support of my children and close friends, I could begin to look ahead rather than over my shoulder. I was free to be me, unconstrained by any image of the past.

I had my life all planned "from here to eternity." I moved to a very nice upscale retirement center. I made friends with whom I shared stories about children and grandchildren. I joined them for in-house social events, and went with them to church and community events. Soon I joined a fitness center, found a new support group in water aerobics, and chose a new hair salon. Two years passed by.

Then, one day my hair stylist mentioned he had a client, a widower, he would like me to meet. Phooey! The last thing I had in mind was another male in my life! Since I saw my years as limited, I had actually been choosing music to be played at my memorial service, so I said an emphatic, "No, thank you!"

Throughout the next year, two *seasoned* citizens continued spinning in their separate orbits.

He says:

Our hair stylist took up the mantle of matchmaker. He knew me from the years I brought in my invalid wife and from my own occasional haircuts.

One day he asked, "Are you going out since your wife's death?"

"Some" was my reluctant answer. The hairdresser replied, "I have a client you really should meet. If I gave you her phone number, would you call her?"

Without enthusiasm I said, "Why not?

She says:

Throughout the next year, the hairstylist kept insisting this fellow and I had a lot in common. Each of us had served as college fundraisers, and we had both been active in local community theaters. He said our love for musicals and drama was the same, we were very supportive of non-profits and their purpose, and we were both involved alumni of our universities. Each had four adult children and lots of grandchildren. Even great grandchildren! The hairstylist also said, "I guarantee you...he is one of the nicest men in this community."

Finally I gave in, allowing my private telephone number to be given to this gentleman. This was such a new thing for me; my expectations were low. Surprisingly, he called. He introduced himself, finally putting a name to the mystery. He said he would like to meet me, and promised to call when he returned from a long anticipated cruise on the Mississippi River with family. I had my own plans for an Alaska trip with family.

I said, "That would be nice," secretly doubting I would hear from him and not caring much.

Date # 1: He did call! This time he was preoccupied with a grandson who was hospitalized. Excuses, excuses, excuses! I didn't really care. But soon, he called again to invite me to have lunch with him. I accepted. Lunch is a safe date for it can be ended quickly or enjoyed at leisure. He offered me the option of coming by for me, or meeting me at the restaurant. I chose the first.

How would I know him? He told me he would be in a red Cadillac with OU Sooners stickers. Uh, oh! My car showed several OSU Cowboy stickers! There is no greater rivalry in Oklahoma then between my beloved Oklahoma State University and his University of Oklahoma.

The lunch was rather fun. Nice place, good food, great ambiance. We had no trouble getting to know one another. We found that we both attended OU at the same time: 1952-54, then I transferred to OSU. One hour stretched to two. He said he would like to see me again. My thoughts were "maybe."

Date # 2: Before long he did call to invite me to a concert being performed at the church we both attend. It's a big church and we had never seen one another there. Again, this sounded like a safe date. It was on a Wednesday night, no conflict with my girlfriends, so I accepted. How much difficulty can you get into on a church date?

Afterwards we went to a restaurant for a bite to eat. As we sat there, we began to share the amusing advice we were receiving from our family members about getting back into the dating game. We laughed so much we didn't realize the place was closing. The staff was sweeping the floor and told us we were having so much fun, they didn't want to interrupt us.

Date #3: The retirement center where I live sent invitations to all old codgers living in our zip code to be guests at a "Margaritaville" party. He asked if I would be there. Upon my wholehearted reply of "yes," he said, "I'll see you there!"

During this hilarious evening, I asked him to join the table with several of my lady friends. After the evening was over, my friends evaluated the match up. Apparently the two of us had an immediate aura of happiness and my friends approved enthusiastically. He had passed his first test!

Date #4: Later he called to ask me to dinner and to see the Lyric Theatre production of "Call Me Madam." I said yes because I do love musical theater. I went shopping and bought a new ankle-length skirt. Even at my age, I felt all pretty and feminine.

He says:

Dinner at the OKC Museum of Art Cafe was delightful. The show was fantastic. But between the two, we had to walk across a construction zone that looked like photos of Berlin after WWII. I wish we had a video of these octogenarians helping one another from one rock pile to another. Strangely, what could have been an annoyance became a comical adventure to be shared.

She says:

I enjoyed being with him on these first dates. He is somewhat old-fashioned about opening car doors, helping with my coat, and pulling out chairs, all of which took some getting used to. After all, I was now a free and independent woman! However, this renewed custom makes me feel very special and he could feel gallant again.

Thus it began, thus it continues. Somehow I am no longer concerned what hymns are sung, what music is played, or who plays it when I die. I am more concerned with living!

"Some Enchanted Evening"

He says:

Maybe some of you are like we were.

We weren't looking for romance. We had reconciled ourselves to being Grandpa or Nana; we had accepted our individual lives on the sidelines. We were included at family gatherings and made over on our birthdays. We traveled, but there is nothing lonelier than traveling alone.

We were both active in church and civic organizations. But it is a couple's world. The odd man or woman soon feels left out, an intruder in the happy times of others. "Table for One" is the loneliest phrase in our language.

"Some Enchanted Evening" or morning or noon, you meet a special someone and sparks fly. Perhaps you were introduced by a friend, or met at church, a community event, etc. Part of your brain that had grown rusty from inactivity suddenly kicks into gear with the old rating system:

Appearance - attractive
Personality - pleasant
Disposition - laughs a lot

Then you talk. You might go together for coffee or lunch, or just banter back and forth as you participate in activities.

Now you begin to notice other things:

Voice – pleasing
Brain - seems to be in gear before mouth opens

Shared interests:

Music
Theater
School and church ties
Movies
Kids, grand kids, and even great grand kids

Unthinking, you proceed down the list of what you would look for, if you were looking. But you're not looking; you know better than that.

Both of you find you are using a different scale of attractiveness than when you were younger. Physical perfection is out, eyes are in! No longer bound by the genetic need to find a mate to procreate and nurture offspring, you notice the eyes—which are the windows of the soul, **smile lines** around the mouth, and **gentle hands** with a tender touch.

Then it happens! You want to be friends or even more than friends. You want romance. Not casual, but genuine romance. WHAM, BAM, ALAKAZAM!

She says:

Everyone exhorts you to be cautious. "What do you know about him? What about his family? What about your family? You know you can have your heart broken. Go slow and be careful!"

He says:

Being too careful can be lonely. Couples have fun that is denied singles. Scientific studies have shown conclusively: shared joy is sweeter; shared loss more bearable, shared fear less terrible, and shared hope more beautiful. My heart agrees.

In these latter years, I realized it wasn't about finding a lover. I longed for someone who would share my interests, someone who didn't see the world through widow's eyes by focusing on the past, and someone to hold up in my mind's eye when I listened to my favorite romantic songs and greeted the evening hours of loneliness. I yearned for someone to touch and to hold, to have healthy discussions about current events and family changes, and to be my companion as we face the uncertainties of tomorrow and the excitement of living each day to its fullest.

I am grateful I allowed myself to renew the sparkle in my eyes and the spring in my step, and that I wasn't too careful!

"Getting To Know You"

She says:

It was not long after those first dates that Bob asked me to go to Texas with him to attend, of all things, a reunion of his late wife's family. Where I found the courage I don't know, but I agreed.

We flew into Houston and rented a car to go to Brazoria for the festivities. I was somewhat amazed to find that Bob was held in such warm regard by his in-laws. He was still very much a part of this big rowdy Irish clan. Their affection toward him carried over to me. I was received with courtesy and warmth.

It was on the flight back to Oklahoma City that Bob shocked me by saying, over the roar of the jet engines, "I want you to know that I intend to be a part of your life from now on."

I was not ready for this! I was flattered, but frightened. I vowed to myself to take it slow and easy.

He says:

I surprised myself, too. I have always "played my cards close to my vest" to avoid the possible turn down. Now, here I was promising (or threatening) a long-term relationship. The truth was, and still is, that I liked what I saw in her.

I had no time, or inclination, to play a waiting game. I went into courtship mode.

She says:

He was very attentive. I found myself receiving short stories and song parodies he wrote such as "Courting Miss Mona," "A Funny Thing Happened on the Way to Eternity," and "Walmart in the Rain." They were clever and fun. Then to my great surprise I realized he was saying things I was feeling, but had no words to describe. There grew an intimacy of spirit that I called being soul mates. I actually bought and sent the same Hallmark card to him on two occasions celebrating that we were rapidly becoming soul mates.

He says:

What fun! There was a junior high school flavor to this romance. If she had books, I would have carried them for her. Both her friends and mine saw the aura of gladness that surrounded us, and smiled with approval.

"Without a Song"

He says:

Mona and I both like music, especially show tunes and "Golden Oldies." She produced community musicals as fund raisers for non-profits for many years. I know the lyrics to scores of songs but am challenged by a tin ear. I often say I burst into song, for I never have the right key. While traveling in the car, what a team we are, as she keeps me on tune and I keep us on the correct words while we sing to tunes of the past.

In keeping with the junior high aspect of our budding romance, we had to have a special song, one that would now and forever be ours.

She says:

More fun for us! We combed our memories for songs with special meaning. We rather liked "Cherish" until we got all the lyrics. Then Bob cast a veto. "That is a loser's song. He is whining because she chose the other fellow. I don't intend to lose!"

He says:

We played with this problem for weeks. How blessed we are that choosing our song should be our greatest concern. Then one evening on the radio, an obscure Frank Sinatra tune, "This Happy Madness" was played. It was perfect!

It tells our story. It has a lilting happy tune. Its very obscurity makes it all the more ours. It even hints at divine intervention, something we have suspected all along.

"This Happy Madness"

What should I call this happy madness
that I feel inside of me?
Some time of wild October gladness
that I thought I'd never see.
What has become of all my sadness,
all my endless lonely sighs?
Where are my sorrows now?

What happened to my frown
and is that self-contented clown,
Standing there grinning in the mirror really me?
I'd like to run through Central Park,
carve your initials in the bark,
Of every tree for everyone to see.

I feel that I've gone back to childhood,
And I'm skipping through the wildwood.
So excited I don't know what to do.
What do I care if I am juvenile?
I smile my secret little smile,

Because I know the change in me is you.

What shall I call this happy madness,
all this unexpected joy,
That turned my world into a baby's bouncing toy?
The gods are laughing up above,
one of them gave me a little shove,
And I fell gaily, gladly, madly into love.

— Composer Antonio Carlos Jobim
Album: Sinatra and Company

"Someone to Watch Over Me"

He says:

I didn't need anyone. I was in reasonably good health for an octogenarian. I was pleased with the devotion I had given to my deceased wife. I cooked a little. I had no responsibilities. I didn't want anyone. I was free.

Then I met someone...a very special someone with whom I enjoy talking, laughing, and just spending time together. We share common interests, private jokes, our dreams, our joys and our woes. It is absolutely great. I thrill to her touch. I call her each morning to hear her voice. I still don't really need anyone, but I am eternally grateful that I have someone. It is like awakening to a new day.

She says:

I definitely treasured my newfound independence. I felt safe with attentive and caring children and many new friends. I didn't need anyone. I didn't want anyone.

Then out of nowhere I met someone. We have fun. We laugh a lot. He helps me look on the bright side of all the cares of the day. He gently urges me out of the shell where I retreat when negative memories pop up.

He says:

Many of you may say you don't want or need anyone. You are capable of living alone, you drive a car, and you enjoy personal hobbies. That may be.

However, the difference between anyone and *someone* is as vast as the heavens above. A *someone* will be a close friend and an ear to hear your whispered thoughts, who will offer a warm comforting touch and give an encouraging word. A *someone* will say, "It's going to be okay" and help you deal with life's challenges.

They both say:

I didn't want *anyone,* but I am so happy now that I have *someone.*

"Accentuate the Positive"

He says:

I love my lady.

That said, I also love God, my family, my country, Oklahoma University Sooner sports, and rainbow sherbet. The English language has only one word for love. The Greeks had four to differentiate between the different facets of the emotion.

Love wears many guises. There is possessive love, obsessive love, erotic love, brotherly love, altruistic love and adoration. Some are beautiful, some are ugly, and some are downright sick.

So, what do I mean when I say I love my lady? The poet, Liz Browning, wanted to let her man know how she felt: "How do I love thee? Let me count the ways," she wrote. "I love thee to the length and breadth and depth my soul can reach."

Beautiful words, lovely sentiment, but a little ethereal for me. I prefer to be a little more specific: I admire, appreciate, value, and cherish her.

I **admire** her many talents, her indomitable yet gentle spirit, her can-do attitude.

I **appreciate** her character, her sense of values, her honesty and candor, and that she's a woman of many talents who has achieved much in her life.

I **value** her for the warmth and compassion she shows others, her loyalty to friends and family.

I **cherish** our almost metaphysical connection. We laugh at the same things, are moved with like emotions, sense each other's reactions to the happenings of the day. We don't always think alike. We do listen to the other's thoughts, and we respect the other's right to have a differing opinion.

Like most males of my generation I have a "big Daddy" complex; a compulsion to be provider, protector, psychiatrist, and philosopher for all those I love. I can spoil a relationship in the blink of an eye. I have to rein in my inclination to be, "the source of all wisdom, the all-powerful OZ." It is a challenge. If my powers of philosophy are as lacking as my prowess at plumbing, I could quickly create a catastrophe.

To give and to receive love that accentuates the positive is comfortable, is beautiful, and satisfies the soul.

We are surrounded by negativity. The newspaper, the television, and the radio strive to outdo one another in announcing crimes, crises, and catastrophes. There is too much complaining, faultfinding, and general dissatisfaction with life. I want our relationship to concentrate on the things that are good - to value what we have rather than mourn for what we have not. This is true whether we had it and lost it (age does that) or never had it at all.

I am an incurable romantic. I do not apologize for it. I hoard precious memories the way a miser hoards gold. Even disappointments can be recast to become memorable.

A case in point:

We planned an early spring getaway. We would fly into Washington, DC. There we would rent a car and drive to Colonial Williamsburg to spend several days. Then we would return to the Capitol, enjoy the Cherry Blossom Festival, take a moonlight dinner cruise on the Potomac and visit a granddaughter who was working there. We planned early, so we could think of spring and cherry blossoms while the cold Oklahoma wind howled outside.

Sounds romantic doesn't it?

However, an unseasonal cold spell kept the cherry trees from blooming, the young lady we planned to visit had moved back home, and it snowed forcibly on our moonlight dinner cruise.

Did it spoil our outing?

No way! We enjoyed every minute. I will always treasure the memory of the Capitol city in the snow. Soft flakes spiraling down like goose feathers veiling the buildings and monuments. I told you I am a hopeless romantic.

She says:

Dealing with a hopeless romantic who also fashions himself as a man full of malarkey has its challenges. I have always been highly goal oriented. He pushes toward the goal, but stops to sniff flowers along the way. He enjoys the journey, while I'm used to pushing toward the destination. That has sometimes been hard for me, yet I've learned to appreciate the little pleasures.

As a romantic he pays attention to details, special occasions, and anniversaries. We have celebrated anniversaries I had forgotten were milestones in our relationship. For my 81st birthday, before taking me out for a wonderful dinner, he presented me with a gift sack containing a small container of ready-to-eat green grapes, blueberries, cherries and the sweetest raspberries. What better gift to someone who doesn't need much else in life?

Do you remember the song "People Will Say We're in Love" from the stage play Oklahoma? Laurie and Curly gazed lovingly into each other's eyes as they sang about their newfound love. I actually sang Laurie's part in a community program in the 1960's. I never would have dreamed that over 50 years later I would find myself randomly humming this classic song, feeling the same inner joy as Laurie.

I resisted it, but I do love this man. He has pried open parts of my heart I had forgotten existed. My special man tunes in on my emotions, even when I do not verbalize them and he always makes me feel I am special to him. He touches my soul and revives my spirit. I feel cherished; I still can't believe I found this kind of love...in my 80s!

"September Song"

He says:

The years haven't been kind to us. They never are. A glance into the mirror leads us to wonder just who that old person is, staring back so intently. Stairs are steeper, bedtime rolls around an hour or so earlier, and an afternoon nap is a treat, as well as a treatment.

Forget it! We are what we are, not what we were. We might not fare well at the dance marathon, but we will be applauded if we get up and try. So what if my *noble brow* now stretches to between my ears and my *six-pack* abs now more resemble a *pony keg*. We are alive! We have successfully completed many decades. Like the woodsman's axe that had gone through five new handles and three new heads, we have persevered!

Each of us has a unique personality. The proper blending of two makes the sunshine seem brighter. Those old songs we hear on the elevator suddenly have a special meaning, and we even remember the words!

What are the odds of an accomplished lady just turned 79, and a stodgy 80-year old widower entering into a pulse pounding, breathtaking, hilarious romance? The odds makers in Vegas would be pulling out their hair attempting to figure that one. Yet, it happened.

I think that a benevolent God, with a sense of humor, looked down and saw two individuals, too proud and stubborn to admit they were lonely, and decided to put them together and watch what would happen.

We have known each other only two years, yet we find we think of the same things at the same time. Often as not we know exactly what the other's reaction will be to something seen, said, or done. It is eerie, but wonderful.

We can't spend too much time worrying about what others think! To most of the world, we are irrelevant. If we are noticed at all, it is for a brief moment.

We are amazed at the number of people—young and old—who smile as they observe our glow of happiness as we move down the street holding hands. As our relationship develops, the skies seem a more vivid blue, the birds sing more sweetly, the sunshine is brighter, and old songs have new meaning. Each day brings a new promise.

Old age frees us from the burden of peer pressure. We have already outlived most of our peers. The rest won't remember.

This is true freedom.

She says:

My sweetheart and I will do the things we can—together. Shared pleasures are so much sweeter. If we concentrate on what we can do, those things we can no longer do become less important and negligible.

He says:

Late life romance is like Texas Hold'em Poker. If you like the cards you're dealt, you had better be willing to go all in because you don't know how many hands you have left to play.

Cupid's arrow upsets the status quo, destroys habit patterns, and boosts folks out of their ruts, adding pleasure and excitement, even in the 80s and 90s age bracket.

She says:

When women share feelings we only want a listening ear. We are not asking for the man to fix the situation as men so often assume. My new companion immediately became adept in listening and I reciprocated.

It is so nice to become acquainted with this new "real" person, residing inside the body we see. We begin to understand one another on a deeper level, which has been defined by our relationship with family, our spirituality, and how we feel about service to others. We see that we have some of the same philosophies of life. How wonderful to find this!

As we spend time together and see the sameness, we also find differences.

Little things: He will put the dishes in the dishwasher not exactly the way I do. I accept it. This is no time to quibble about who is right. At least he is trying to help. In this new loving friendship, we can remain individuals, while understanding and accepting our differences. We concentrate on the positive things between us, and let the others go. At this age, we know what is important.

He admittedly brings malarkey into our lives, which was suspect at first. He likes to add interesting facts and humor to our conversations. I accepted this as part of him and took it lightly, thinking he was trying to impress me.

I have lived as a poised mother, wife, career woman, and honored volunteer with not much time for foolishness. For years I have had in my possession a Chinese Proverb, *Key to Life's Zest* by Josephine Lowman. I liked what I read, and meant to someday look into the real meaning. Now is that time.

I quote Josephine:

>*"There is great wisdom in foolishness.*
>*It refreshes daily life. There is wisdom in a happy*
>*heart and optimistic outlook. These reflect a zest*
>*for living and a warm outgoing spirit.*
>*Those who have learned the wisdom of foolishness*
>*have gotten life into focus so that the important*
>*values stand out and the others are dimmed."*

This describes my new companion and a new dimension in my everyday life. What fun we have!

He makes a point of making me feel cherished each day. When I bring up a past frustration, he treats it with sincerity and a touch of humor, and steers me toward realizing it is a sheer bonus just to be alive and enjoying the present day. His sunny spirit illuminates my own radiance.

"Yesterday"

He says:

Part of being a *seasoned citizen* is that life has left us with scars....some obvious, some hidden. Crucial to late life romance is how we deal with these hidden hurts.

Watch for over-reaction to some action or word that may have been meant innocently, but triggers a disproportionate response. If it happens, and chances are it will, apologize—mean it—and put that word or action in quarantine.

If you hit that trigger on purpose, you deserve what you get!

On the other hand, you have triggers of your own. Give your partner a break. Assume innocence. At no other time is it more important to have the assumption of innocence until guilt is proven.

It is all right to talk about your triggers and hers. At this age, we are unlikely to achieve much change in the other. At any age all we can really change is our self. But, out of respect, we can learn to avoid arousing the other's painful memories.

The "Banana Incident" was a learning experience early in our relationship. It began innocently enough. I was picking her up to go to the nine o'clock church service.

As usual she was dressed and ready, looking smart and stylish. I asked if she had slept well. She had. I asked if she had breakfast. She had not.

"You really should put something in your stomach," I said. "Breakfast is the most important meal of the day."

Suddenly, it was as if a dark cloud had interrupted a sunny day.

She said nothing as we went to the car. We chatted as we drove, parked and rode the small bus to the church door. All seemed normal. Yet under the surface, ticking like a time bomb, was my concern that she had no breakfast. I later realized this was not the only bomb ticking.

We were in the habit of enjoying a cup of coffee while meeting new people before church began. For this time of socializing, snacks are available: pigs in a blanket, bagel, doughnuts and fruit...lovely yellow bananas.

"Would you like a banana?" I asked.

"No, thank you." she answered.

Tick....tick....tick.

"You really should eat something," I insisted.

"No, thank you," she replied.

Tick....tick....tick.

She went to get coffee, found a seat, and was sipping her drink.

I got in line, purchased a banana, and approached her, banana in hand.

"This should hold you 'til lunch," I said.

Smiling graciously, she ate the banana.

TICK TOCK....

TICK TOCK....

TICK TOCK...

DANGER, DANGER, DANGER.

I need to go into DANGER CONTROL before there is an explosion!

I'm thinking, "What damage control? She is smiling and eating the banana."

Damage Control: Look at those eyes, you idiot! The warm blue you so admire has taken the hue of glacial ice.

She says:

I was thinking, "a darn chauvinistic male! You are not my parent. I hoped better from you. I am eating this fruit because I am a lady and do not wish to cause a scene. But, more than a lady, I am an adult, a woman of achievement, and I will not be ordered about like a child." But I didn't say a thing to him.

He says:

Damage Control: My foot is in my mouth about halfway down to the ankle. It is time to back off and apologize. But what should I apologize for? I was only trying to do what's best for her. I wonder, however, why she is getting quieter and quieter?

Damage Control: My motive was admirable, but method was abominable. Apologize or face the consequence. You have just accomplished an "oh, shit." You have earned several "attaboys," but as you well know, one "oh, shit" completely wipes out a dozen "attaboys."

On the way home, I (reluctantly) said: "I'm sorry if I was out of line about your eating breakfast. I am concerned about you."

"It's okay," she told me demurely.

She says:

I said to myself, "You just blew it, Buster!"

He says:

Damage Control: You can't undo it, you can't hide it. Don't allow it to fester. Your only option is to make a joke of it. Play it up so that when it is recalled, it will bring a smile rather than a frown.

So it became a part of our story. I admit to the world that I was far out of line. She has accepted my apology and now knows that I recognize her independence as I become even more attentive. **All is well.**

They say:

Sometimes the past rises up like a zombie from the grave. Old hurts, old resentments, old fears crowd in. How sweet it is to have someone who not only puts them to flight, but replaces them with good memories, happy times, accomplishments, and goals attained. "It takes a heap of living to make a house a home," said Edgar A. Guest. That heap of living shapes and molds each of us. Moments of nostalgia are to be enjoyed as well as feared.

Both of us had been married to our spouses more than 50 years. Both had raised families with all the attendant craziness that goes with that process. Both are veterans of the dashed hopes, broken dreams, and painful recoveries that life brings. We are also able to look back on the countless happy times, achievements and triumphs that form the tapestry of old age.

Travel is so broadening. We have grown together and closer to each other through the experiences we've shared. Here we admire sand art in Rostock, Germany.

Check hot air balloon ride off the bucket list. We enjoy helping each other fulfill long-time dreams. Our balloon ride was over Las Vegas in 2012.

Atop the Devon Tower in downtown Oklahoma City at Vast Restaurant celebrating the 2nd anniversary of our first date.

*"All I ask is a tall ship and a star to steer her by." –
Sea Fever by John Masefield. Bob captains the yawl,
owned by Mona's son-in-law, down the Indian River in
Florida.*

On our trip to Washington D.C. nothing went as planned. The cherry trees didn't bloom, and it snowed on our dinner cruise of the Potomac. We had a wonderful time anyway.

We joined Lifelong Learning participants on an "Enrichment Voyage" through the Baltic Sea and into the North Atlantic. Aboard we studied oceanography, architecture, history, the arts, and creative writing. Here we are on our way to the Captain's dinner.

When in Orlando one must pay tribute to Mickey Mouse. Bob wanted to check the progress of his courtship; so he bought two T-shirts, one yellow for caution, one green for go and let Mona make her choice.

There was no RED option!

Bob accompanied Mona to the Margaritaville Party hosted by the retirement community where Mona lives. It was date number three and he passed muster with all of Mona's friends.

Lord Robert and Lady Mona at Medieval Times Dinner Show in Orlando. While the armored knights and fair ladies celebrated the romance of King Arthur and Guinevere, we celebrated our own blossoming romance.

Putting on the Ritz at the Adams banquet at the University of Oklahoma. Bob sponsors academic scholarships. At this banquet, the recipients get to meet the donor.

Another scholarship presentation to a special education student at the University of Central Oklahoma. Eighteen different scholarships are given to four area universities by the Aldridge Foundation.

Bob takes great pride in awarding the Aldridge Scholarship. Here he poses with a recipient at the University of Oklahoma Health Science Center.

The way to a lady's heart is through her stomach. Bob impresses Mona with a homemade lunch.

In Lithuania our tour took us to the home of a former British diplomat who had married a Lithuanian lady, and lived in the country.

We loved our visit to Iceland. Together we marveled at the beautiful scenery and enjoyed the friendly folks we met.

The dashing look is courtesy of the new sun glasses, a gift from Mona.

While digging for our roots it was fun to find Aldridge Village, a suburb of Birmingham, United Kingdom.

Double trouble: Mona finds her hands full with Bob's twin great grandsons.

We both enjoy spending time with our families. Here we are in Orlando, Florida with Stacia, Mona's daughter and Tom, Bob's son in December of 2012.

*Wherever we go together feels adventurous and the
Kennedy Space Center did not disappoint. We enjoyed
learning about space travel as much as the young
visitors in Cape Canaveral, Florida.*

Bob's surgery slowed our travel for a bit, but not our adventure. Just spending time together is engaging, laughter-filled, and interesting.

We love this picture. Both of us look good and it causes us to recall a lovely evening we spent together. We attended a banquet for non-profit organizations funded by The Aldridge Foundation.

"Get Happy"

He says:

How sweet it is to laugh together! Shared laughter is more intoxicating than booze. Laugh at life, because life is funny. Laugh together at yourselves, at your clumsy attempts at the techniques of romance. When I get a newspaper, I glance at the headlines, then check the obituaries. If my name is not there, I go to the comics. Some artists hold a mirror to life that evokes your own memories and makes you laugh.

"A merry heart is like good medicine." Shared laughter promotes empathy. Empathy is a cornerstone of romance. To see with her eyes, hear with her ears, and share the feelings of her heart.

I really don't have a clue as to how I should behave. I have never been 80-years old before. This leaves two options: Be what I am, or play an unscripted role as the elderly romantic. I choose to be me. Maybe me polished smooth by wear, but nevertheless, me.

There is no put on between us. We are honest about our emotions. We keep no secrets, hide no imperfections. We share our hopes and fears. We trust. We communicate. I take her into my head as well as my arms. I make room in my heart for her and those she loves.

We are in uncharted territory. No one knows how much time will be allowed us. Our hours together rush by like seconds. Our time apart seems long and dreary.

Do we dare to make ourselves vulnerable again to the pain of a lost love? The calendar will not be denied. Will the memories we make today see us through tomorrow's sadness? It takes a conscious decision. We have made ours.

We shall take the advice of old Omar Khayyam:

Into the fire of Spring
The Winter garment of repentance fling.
For the bird of time has but a moment to flutter
And, lo, the bird is on the wing.

She says:

After you learn to laugh together, you may learn to cry together. There are things in our lives that merit tears. We lose old friends. We might face illness, disability, and dementia, our own and those we love. Disappointments may abound.

Shared tears also build empathy. They help bridge the gap between his views and mine. Men and women see the same event differently. Empathy spans that difference.

He says:

There is no place in our romance for the "Macho Man" who hides his emotions or the "Sturdy Oak" who stands alone against the storms of life. **We share our vulnerability.**

"That's Life"

He says:

So, there we were. Our relationship was growing stronger and more comfortable daily. Life was a walk in the park. Then we were met by a mugger. Its name was **cancer.**

That's life, after all; even the Garden of Eden had this talking snake.

It began with a routine visit to my urologist. I thought I was having another bout with kidney stones. After x-rays he told me that I should have a cystoscopy, an exploratory procedure.

What? Me worry? Not I. I advised my children in a way least inclined to produce panic. Shortly before Labor Day with both my sons and Mona in attendance, I underwent the procedure. The doctor found cancer, re-sectioned my bladder, and removed the cancer.

She says:

Upon hearing the word, cancer, my mind slipped quickly into a state of confusion. I wondered what this would mean for us. Will he suffer much during this time of recovery? How will he accept this new phase in his life? Will he be able to be with me often? Just what is my role in this health crisis? Is there a place for me in the family decisions?

He says:

The pathology report was reassuring. We caught it early. It was stage one and had not spread.

I was eager to return to my present lifestyle, which certainly included Mona. I planned a trip to Florida for us to celebrate Thanksgiving with son, Tom, and granddaughter, Katie. We left Oklahoma City in an ice storm and endured unseasonable cold in Florida. Even so, we had a wonderful time just being together.

Returning to Oklahoma City I checked in for a follow-up on the surgery. More complications! I flunked my EKG before the surgery. The doctors sent me to my cardiologist, who recommended I get a pacemaker. Another invasive operation.

She says:

I had only been to Bob's home a few times during our first year together. Early in the relationship, I had to be *vetted* by his canine companion, a Shih Tzu who has been his fuzzy buddy for ten years. That went well. The home was filled with family mementos and pictures of Bob and his late wife. I treaded softly, not wanting to encroach upon those memories. I wanted to be there for Bob, but not to crowd out his children, who surrounded him with affection and caring after his surgeries. I still hadn't figured out my role. I missed the companionship. I missed his happy countenance. I missed the touch of his hand in mine.

He says:

I got my pacemaker the day after Christmas. January was its *shakedown cruise* or evaluation period. Once I was cleared by the cardiologist, I got back on the schedule for the urology follow-up that was postponed in December.

This one turned out to be scary. The surgeon thought the cancer had reoccurred. When he reported to Mona and my son, Rusty, it scared them speechless. Thanks be to God, to medical science, and to the prayers of family and friends, this was not so. Pathology reported it was just scar tissue.

Again I tried to get back to my old routine. I signed up for the February Lifelong Learning classes alongside Mona. On February 27, I thought I was having a stroke. I had been reading my newspaper; but when I stood up my legs would not support me. I fell kerplop.

Scolding myself, I said "Old fool, you stood too fast. At your age you don't need booze, just standing too fast gets the same effect!" Standing more slowly did not help. I went kerplop again!

I went over the stroke symptoms I knew. Not a stroke, but what was it?

We went to the emergency room where doctors soon diagnosed I had a toxic buildup of potassium due to kidney failure.

Now, that was scary. Kidney failure sounds like a death sentence. It isn't. In medical terms, any less than 100%, is considered failure. I would have much preferred to call it a malfunction. Anyway I underwent dialysis to clean my blood and yet another procedure to insert a stent between kidney and bladder to keep things flowing.

It was a crazy time. The winter weather was so bad, schools were closed. Three doctors were making decisions about my treatment, but no one was talking to the nurses, to the family, nor to me. We were concerned and frightened. Then Mona took charge! Like a fully rigged man-of-war going into battle, she met the crisis head on; and she prevailed. I have no idea what she said or to whom, but she cut through red tape and protocol like a hot knife cuts butter.

She says:

To my amazement, throughout all the medical issues Bob maintained the same positive outlook every minute of every day: calm, pleasant, loving, and even jovial. He continued to be the rock for his family, friends, and especially me.

He says:

By the time I had still another procedure, to remove the stent, I had spent seven months in and out of hospitals, had five surgical procedures and compiled more sick time than in the previous eighty-one years.

How lucky I am to have Mona at my side. Unobtrusively, she was the anchor that kept my children from drifting into panic and me from falling into the depths of self-pity.

She says:

We persevered though these seven months of crisis still committed to one another: a commitment that deepened whether we were together or forced apart by circumstances.

It has made us increasingly aware of how short the time together may be.

"Far Away Places"

He says:

Was it simply a vacation, an opportunity to escape for a while, an odyssey, an educational experience, or an experiment in togetherness? It was all of these.

It was Semester at Sea's Enrichment Voyage 2014. For twenty-eight days we sailed the Baltic, then the North Sea. We visited twelve countries. We heard scholarly presentations in oceanography, political science, architecture, medicine, and the arts. We met folks from every corner of the United States plus Canadians and Australians. We shared tables with people of varied ages, from college kids to those in their nineties. We rode many buses, climbed countless stairs, and ate foods we had never tasted.

Mostly, however, whether or not it was the objective of the journey, we saw one another unmasked.

She was treated to my wake-up call of twelve hearty sneezes every morning. We reached an agreement that all talking was to be kept to the essentials until we had drunk at least one cup of coffee.

I saw her with her hair down, without make-up, and on occasion about half seasick. It is not easy to be glamorous when your stomach is doing flips.

We have been asked, countless times, "How did you get along?" My answer is that we got along like two people who are fond enough of one another to overlook one another's foibles and eccentricities. We shared our opinions of the classes, of the entertainment, of the food, and, yes, of the people we met.

There were two fabulous ladies, both walking with canes, who never let their disabilities keep them from seeing everything there was to see; one gentleman who walked with two canes but kept smiling as he struggled along. There was the "sweat lodge lady" who thought she knew it all about Native Americans and proceeded to tell us about our Oklahoma tribes. Some were fun to be with, some were not.

We noticed Father Time is a sculptor who works in human flesh. Some faces we saw had been molded into permanent smile lines. Others looked as if they had been weaned on sour pickles. It seems to boil down to a question of attitude. Some see the glass half full; others see it half empty. Some don't even see the glass.

She says:

I was concerned about how he would like this trip. Two of my children and two grandchildren had been on the regular Semester at Sea voyages. After a grandson said "Nana, why don't you go on one of their Enrichment Voyages?", I did go on one three years ago and I loved it. How happy it made me to see my man comfortable in this learning atmosphere.

We were great companions during this trip. I found that he enjoys spending time reading novels (of all kinds) as I do...compatibility seemed to increase in many new areas as we traveled.

During our meals on the ship, we chose to eat in the formal dining room, where we would be seated at tables of four, six, or even eight. We were fascinated by the life stories of our new friends from all over the world.

While observing my man as we interacted daily with many different nationalities and ages, I came to the awareness that he is **culturally astute!** I was constantly surprised and somewhat awed at the range and amount of data he remembers...the who, what, when, and where of history, geography, finance, political leadership, music, art and drama, not only for our own country, but for countries around the world. He even knows the location of well-known restaurants and what food and beverages they serve. He has obtained this knowledge and experience from the travels he shared with his own family, and keeping abreast of such information from National Geographic Magazine, TV travel shows, and the like.

The term culturally astute has been described as "building bridges with all kinds of people and building relationships with deep connections." I have always marveled at Bob's natural abilities to connect with others, but this trip brought a new appreciation as I witnessed his immediate connection with strangers from throughout the world. Others are drawn to his warmth, humor, and genuine concern for others. It makes me so proud to be his special lady!

"The Best Things in Life are Free"

He says:

Oil and water do not mix. My family has its own dynamics as does hers. The most important thing the families have in common is their heartfelt desire to see their Nana and Pa find some happiness.

Oil and water can be emulsified. Both retain their character but they form a new compound. It can happen to families in a similar way.

If Nana seems happy—Pa is accorded acceptance, then respect, and finally affection. If Pa shows a new zest for life and sports a happy smile, Nana is welcomed into the fold.

There are boundaries beyond which neither Nana nor Pa would dare go. Every clan has its problems; problems that must be addressed jointly. However, some solutions may need to be addressed individually, with support being given quietly from the sidelines.

There are always financial considerations. We live in a society complicated by eli-
gibility for Social Security, Medicare, and pen-
sions, plus boundaries set by wills, trusts, and
estate plans.

These complications affect all concerned. No
one wants Nana left destitute, nor Pa living on
a pittance. It is challenging to consider what is
theirs, and how to divide their individual assets
among their own family members.

We don't like to talk about these things—we
don't even like to think of them. Realistically,
however, they must be considered. The peace of
mind of all concerned is at stake. We are already
living on borrowed-bonus-time. What happens
when that time runs out? Plan for it together,
and agree on a plan.

We come from a generation where the man
was first among equals. Papa got first choice of
the fried chicken, and the largest slice of pie. He
took responsibility for making a living. It has
marked our generation. We have viewed life
with a "Father knows best" viewpoint.

This was never actually true or fair. It has

taken two generations to realize this. Families have become less autocratic, more democratic.

Now, at this stage of life, a new dynamic appears. Making a living is relegated to endorsing a few checks and watching personal investments. She has become an independent woman, managing her own finances.

It isn't just about money, family pride, and material things. Ideals and aspirations come into play. Is this how I want to be remembered? What is my legacy? These questions get a lot of thought.

Now, I've made it sound terribly complex and challenging, haven't I? It is! But no more so than **life without that touch of a caring hand, or the contentment of being together.** Caring and concern are the tickets to contentment and satisfaction in this new relationship.

"You Brought a New Kind of Love"

He says:

My sweetheart is a book person. She loves to read. She believes that the answers to most of life's most vexing problems can be found between the covers of some book, somewhere. So, as our relationship began to develop, she sought inspiration in the bookstore. (Oh, how I wish I could have been a fly on the wall the day she accidentally picked up a *Kama Sutra book!*) She found a fair number of books that addressed love and romance up to age 70. We wondered about the 80s.

One of her purchases was a scholarly writing that dealt with the frightful changes age causes, physically and mentally. Once we navigated through the first unhappy chapters, we reached the real meat of the treatise: what roles do love and romance have in giving meaning to later life and what advantages do older people bring to the art of love?

We would like to share our experiences in our intimate relationship on two levels: Emotional Intimacy and Physical Intimacy.

On Emotional Intimacy

He says:

There is much debate on what is the most attractive aspect of the young male: physique, hair, eyes, sense of humor, etc. There is no argument on what is the most attractive aspect of the older male. **It is his ears, listening ears.**

Guys, you will be forgiven for thinning hair or a spare tire around your middle if you will learn to listen to your lady.

What are the four words that strike terror to most men?

"We need to talk."

It doesn't have to be this way. Emotional Intimacy is built on trust and understanding. We guys talk a lot. We rattle on about sports, business, politics, hobbies and women. What we don't talk about is feelings.

Women readily share their feelings. We need

to listen. Not just hear her words, but listen for the cues that come from her body language, tone of voice, and choice of words. Just listen!

She has not come to you for a solution. Do not offer one!

She just needs to talk about it. Share her concerns, celebrate her joys. The empathy that develops is delightful. You laugh at the same things, often little private jokes that no one else shares. Your viewpoints may differ, yet each respects the other as an individual and values that different input. She is not your mirror image; she is the other half of the **us** you are creating.

She says:

Physical closeness comes so much easier when there is empathy and trust built through emotional intimacy. It is important to be honest with each other. We are too old to play act to impress.

Living a lie is the hardest work you will ever do. Celebrate your uniqueness as much as what you have in common.

When you and I become **us,** it is magical. A whole new world opens up.

My former life as serious career woman and mother has changed as he carries me—kicking and screaming—into the wonderful world of malarkey and playfulness. He will start with a fact or two, then elaborate, extrapolate, and embroider his facts until his story has taken on a life of its own. He makes me giggle frequently. I was not accustomed to this. I didn't take enough time for fun. Now I do and I love it! And I love him. There is more fun in our lives, yet we still function as well or better than we did when every move was cloaked in seriousness.

On Physical Intimacy

He says:

Science has found that touching is vital in human development. Infants cared for but not cuddled are slower to develop. Other studies have shown this need goes way beyond infancy.

After all, the skin that covers your body is one huge sensory organ. A tender touch can communicate empathy or encouragement better than a thousand words.

We touch. We hold hands in church. We play footsy on the ottoman as we watch television together. People see us walking together holding hands. They smile.

We kiss often and with enthusiasm, whether alone or riding up in the elevator. We kiss hello and goodbye. We hug. She fits very nicely into my arms. She feels comfortable there. I massage her feet. She trims my nails. It is another way of saying, "I care for you."

It has been our observation that true love is largely learned rather than instinctive. It depends upon the ability to recognize and share feelings...and to achieve mutual tenderness and thoughtfulness. This is what we desire in this very meaningful late life romance.

She says:

The romance is exhilarating. I like it. His courtship makes me feel loved, cherished and valued. There is an almost constant stream of little things, a flower plucked from his garden means more to me than a bouquet from a florist. A note, an errand run, his interest in my passion for adult education, and his daily calls all confirm his concern for me.

I believe that the small surprises make the difference in developing a truly romantic relationship. Intimacy carries with it the possibilities for excitement and romance. It celebrates the joy in being alive. Beyond passion, it expresses affection, esteem and loyalty.

They say:

Every couple must work out their own approach to intimacy. The secret is to share feelings with open, honest dialogue. The perspective is newfound in this genuine relationship. Loyalty, respect, and honor. Somehow, these meld into a wonderful intimacy that meets the needs of both. Giving love becomes so much more important than being loved. When both are on this page, the intimacy becomes almost spiritual.

He says:

Intimacy is a celebration of love. As with any celebration, it takes preparation. My lady does not like bristly chins. I make sure that I am cleanly shaved. I dress to please her as she dresses to please me. We both brush our teeth before closeness occurs. That doesn't sound very romantic, you may say. It can be. It is for us.

We talk, we laugh, we touch. We are very close friends as well as devoted partners. We are each conscious of the other's state of mind and physical wellness. Love in the 80s takes on different meaning than love as a young adult.

As the song says, "Little Things Mean a Lot." I open doors for my lady. I pull out her chair at the table. It took several weeks for her to get used to these renewed courtesies. Now, she likes being treated special.

Another song comes to mind, "Try a Little Tenderness." One particular line says, "Love is her whole happiness." I believe this to be true.

This tenderness might be a little gift, a flower, a card, something that shows she is forever in your mind and heart. It doesn't have to be expensive. A single rose for a special occasion can mean more than a bouquet of dozens. Remember special occasions, create them, and revel in the memories.

My special lady was gone to Florida for a few days and I wanted to make her return special. Remembering her saying how she loved home grown radishes from her daddy's garden, I prepared a gift sack with fresh red radishes trimmed and ready to eat (I even tried, without success, to trim them like rose buds.) Her reaction? "It's the funniest and most unusual gift, and I absolutely love it!"

She says:

I am a girl again. Joyously, I am thrilled with romance in this late life! I love the freedom to be in love, to laugh, to snuggle. Snuggling is better than chocolate! The warmth of togetherness, the "just us against the world" feeling is priceless. When he takes me in his arms, a feeling of peace appears. His honeyed words and tender touch are so comforting.

"Love and Marriage"

He says:

This late life romance has come a long way. We have discovered there is a whole new world to experience: new adventures, new joys, and, yes, new problems, too. What is our next step? What options are open to us?

Option One: Get Married

Our generation tended to make marriage a destination rather than a journey together. At our ages, this does not make a lot of sense for us. Our journey together will not change because of "ink stains dried upon some lines." We are committed to each other. The time left to us, be it months or years, is more precious than gold. As mentioned earlier, there are many considerations—some financial, some familial, some legal—that make late life marriage very complicated. We have talked with some for whom marriage has been a wonderful option. Others have said they had a fine romance until they married.

We will choose the option that works best for us in these circumstances.

I am proud of my lady. Nothing would give me more pleasure than introducing her as my wife. She, on the other hand, has been heard to say in jest, "I was a wife for over fifty years. I am enjoying being the girl friend!"

Option Two: Live Together

This option dodges many of the complications that accompany marriage. Two can live more cheaply together than living apart. It has all the advantages of togetherness and mutual support, but with one serious caveat: Is this the way we want to be remembered by our grandchildren?

Maybe there are more important considerations than what our children and grandchildren may think.

We are brain washed. Our generation did not cohabitate, much less shack up. Financial advantages are not so important to us. We have several concerns. For example, should one be hospitalized, the other could not make any decisions as to treatment or even be advised of the condition of the patient. That thought is frightening.

Option Three: Committed Relationship, Living Apart

She jokingly said, "I'll share my life with you, but not my closet!" This option allows each of us to have his or her own space. Though more expensive than living together, it avoids making a decision of whose home becomes the joint residence.

And, let's face it; over the decades we have each accumulated our special stuff that is very meaningful to us but not necessarily to the one we love. This provides space for that special stuff. We have seen this work even when the two lived in different cities, and even different countries.

Every couple must decide among the options based on their own considerations. Each has advantages and disadvantages. Currently we are leaning toward Option Three. I recognize I am at my best when in courtship mode. So, at the present time, why not make it an ongoing courtship wherein she can be the **cherished companion?**

They say:

We are very thankful a new facet of our lives has opened up. What a blessing! Now our thoughts go to what each can contribute in building closeness on a deeper level than ever before. What an opportunity!

We do mellow with years, but we can stay dynamic, curious, and passionate about life. We plan to live each day as if we have eternal life. We have become whole again. We've survived the spring storms and summer droughts of life. **Now, in the twilight of our lives, we pour out our love for each other against the coming cold. In the glow of life's moon, our new love has become an "October Rose."**

Meet the Authors

Bob Aldridge

Bob Aldridge is a born and bred OU Sooner who enjoyed a successful career in retail management with the former C.R. Anthony company after graduating from the University of Oklahoma. Upon retirement he became  a Certified Financial Planner, then transitioned to philanthropist when he started the Aldridge Family Foundation in 1995. Bob takes great personal pride in the successes of college students who have received Aldridge Scholarships in nursing, business, education, fine arts, and science. Bob has authored numerous children's short stories, which are in the process of being published. Family is a priority for Bob, which includes his 4 children, 7 grandchildren, 9 great-grandchildren and 1 great-great-grandchild.

Mona Long

Mona Long is an accomplished fund raising professional and civic volunteer who impacted the lives of thousands by developing new initiatives and raising millions for universities and non profits. A graduate of Oklahoma State University and Phillips University, one of her most significant achievements was the establishment of a statewide Lifelong Learning Program that provides educational opportunities for over 1,000 senior adults annually. In 1979, Mona was recognized as Oklahoma's Mother of the Year, honoring her for outstanding accomplishments throughout the community and state. Mona's primary source of pride is her 4 children, 7 grandchildren and 1 great-grandchild.

Bob and Mona facilitated a seminar, "Late Life Romance," while on the 2014 Semester at Sea Enrichment Voyage to the Baltic Sea. They are available for enlightening and entertaining programs for senior adults who are interested in late life romance and keeping their zest for life.

They may be contacted
at *monalong54@swbell.net.*

Follow Bob and Mona
at *Facebook.com/OctoberRoseTheBook*

CPSIA information can be obtained at www.ICGtesting.com
Printed in the USA
LVOW08s0302071214

417550LV00003B/5/P